STRAW GODS

Tom O'Brien is an Irishman living in London. Amongst other jobs, he's worked as a corporate and creative scriptwriter before moving to prose and specializing in flash fiction. He has words in numerous places including *Ellipsis Zine*, *Reflex Fiction* and *Spelk*, and in print in *Blood & Bourbon, Blink-Ink* and *DEFY!* anthologies. *Straw Gods* was longlisted for the Bath Novella-in-Flash Award and shortlisted by *Ellipsis Zine*.

Straw Gods

Tom O'Brien

REFLEX PRESS

First published in 2020 by Reflex Press
Abingdon, Oxfordshire, OX14 3SY
www.reflex.press

A CIP catalogue record of this book is
available from the British Library.

ISBN: 978-1-9161115-6-1

1 3 5 7 9 10 8 6 4 2

Cover image by Tom O'Brien

www.reflex.press/straw-gods/

For Roz, my first reader

CONTENTS

I Know That You're Dead

'I know that you're dead,' I said to my husband. He didn't respond. I kept my back to him, polishing the glass of the stopped clock. The first time I saw Matteo in its face, I said those words to convince myself. Now they were part of the ritual to bring him back.

Even in the mottled reflection, he looked handsome as he sat at our kitchen table waiting for tea. Beside me the boiling water murmured another rule: 'Don't look at him until you give him the tea, Rosa.'

I ignored it when it hissed, 'If he's there.'

The Purpose of Grief

On the memento shelf there was a pearl he gave me, and a glass dome, a lump of amber, some paper, records, proof he thought of me from far away. I cleaned the old wood with a scarf he slipped over my eyes one night, so I could feel but not see him.

In a bowl of saltwater below the shelf, I kept stones rescued from the beach. The water cooled those stones, filled with pain and memory. It burned off every night, and I changed it every day.

Matteo died, but where was the mercy in giving him up? What was better about never seeing him? In my grief, I had my purpose. I would live with my dead husband or go to him.

There was an order of words when I called him to me, a time of day, actions I took. Once I had a marriage, now I had a ritual.

Little Flag

The first time I saw Matteo in the stopped clock's glass, he was more than a shadow, less than a reflection. Gone when I turned. That flicker was enough. I'd needed a sign he wanted our life as much as I did. He gave me that sign, so I continued our life. We were the husband and wife death couldn't part.

I took the pouch of tea leaves and breathed its scented history before I dipped it in one cup, then the other. Tea stained the water like blood while the room filled with his favourite ginger and lemon. My heart bruised against my ribs and lungs.

Shaking, I spilled tea drops when I faced the table and saw him still there. The soft cry may have come from my mouth or a bird racing the wind, but my lost husband was waiting for me.

I took tightrope steps across my kitchen and placed one cup in front of Matteo then sat opposite him, cradling my own cup in both hands. He was silent, but I chattered enough for us both. 'Some fools are going out in that sea,' I said, nodding to the storm building outside our window.

There was no storm when he drowned. A freak wave hit the boat, they told me, caused by something far away. It left the other man, took my Matteo.

I swallowed my tea and watched him through the steam. His tanned face trembled, and it looked like he was smiling.

That hair would never thin, and no stubble grow to scratch our kisses.

What did he see across the table? A young woman, ageing as he wouldn't. Small, no longer dressed in bright colours, but I let my untimely white hair flow to my shoulders and blow in the wind when I walked on the beach. Rosa, his little flag, guiding him home.

Rough Hands

The rough hands on the smoothed wood table bore the marks of his life, even the dark ring scalded into one finger, burned by a rope that got away. The urge to touch this hand, so close to mine, made my fingers twitch.

Matteo shimmered as if in the steam from his tea and vanished.

'No,' I said, but even his shadow fled, so I pleaded with charged air, cursing that need to touch him, that need for more.

I'd been so careful, built silent walls around the sea of my rage, but waves burst through. 'Straw god,' I said. 'When I pray, you give me nothing but more pain. A space only grief can fill.'

The house shivered in storm winds at my blasphemy.

I breathed the frustration down, and when I steadied my hand, picked up both cups, mine empty, his full.

That's what freed my tears, the brimming cup. A wish couldn't drink tea.

Scream into Thunder

'I didn't walk into the sea last night,' I said to the sky while I washed ginger and desolation from my teacups. We'd set our little cottage far from the village, on a mound that exchanged protection for a view of the horizon, but that question drifted across the bay, smuggled in the scent of family meals, in smoke from burning brush, the sound of children protesting bedtime. Would Rosa walk into the water to join her husband?

'The sand didn't go cold under my feet. It didn't change from dry to wet while I chased the tide. You never grabbed my ankles,' I told the sea, because it asked me too, as did the wind in the endless nights. There was no answer on the cold pillow beside me every morning. 'I did not,' I said. 'I did not.'

The sea called me a liar when it sent silent lightning skittering across its surface on thin violent legs, illuminating the figures on the beach. I recognised my sister and my niece. The mother didn't talk to me; the daughter sneaked over on visits.

Two young men were there too, admiring the thunderheads, standing by their boat as if they dared go fishing in the coming storm. The father of one sat on a boat a decade ago while the sea stole my husband.

The air boomed, and a magnificent shudder ran through my body. The window shivered the figures on the beach. My jars, tins and boxes rattled their displeasure at this disturbance, but it released me. I hid a scream in the thunder, unheard by sea or sky or dead husband.

When the scream died, I whispered in the long echo. 'I made myself this for you. I turned into a wife. You turned me into a widow. I made the home you wanted; you promised to bring the world to me. Now I'm alone.' I'd said too much in a rush and not enough.

I didn't describe the pushing of the sea around my knees last night, because I hadn't gone there. Nor the probing of it around my waist, its power, the push behind me as I neared the shelf that drops away fast and deep. There would be no swimming in my heavy skirts, and I would fall fall fall for him again.

I didn't walk into the sea last night, past that shelf that drops away. But why this morning were my clothes wet?

Shadow-Boxing

Sol danced along the beach in a shadow-boxer's crouch as thunder lumbered to shore. He timed his punches to the lightning drawing fresh bruises on the dawn horizon. Some storms were like an ambush: sudden, tight and violent. This one was like the card at a boxing match, building up to the heavyweight bout.

'The Kid is giving as good as he gets,' his friend Illy said, using his beer bottle as a microphone, with the nasal twang of a radio commentator.

Where Sol was tall and lean, always moving, Illy was a shorter, solid build and steady. As the gusts blew hair into his eyes, he didn't miss a line. 'Not many contenders are brave enough to take on Old Thunder,' he paused. 'Or stupid enough.'

Sol reeled from the imagined force of the blow when a ferocious crack of lightning hammered the sea.

'The champ lands a vicious hook. The Kid is reeling, I can tell you.'

Sol staggered, legs wobbling, fell on his backside.

'The Kid is down,' Illy said. 'He's down. There's no coming back from this. But wait. He's getting up. The count is eight, but he's getting up. I've never seen anything like it. The Kid's taken a battering, but he's back for more. He's on his feet, he's dancing. He throws a left. Throws a right. Those are for show. He's taunting the old champ, toying with him and—' The beach shook with a roar of thunder so powerful it drowned him.

Sol collapsed into laughter and grabbed his own beer from the sand.

'Hey, boys,' came a shout from behind them. 'Best drag your boat off the sand.'

Sol grunted. It was Jacobo, dispensing advice they didn't need. When he turned, he saw the older fisherman dragging his boat to the scruffy wall of palms and mangroves where Agatha, his wife, waited. Trees with boats already lashed to them leaned apart when gusts muscled through, giving a glimpse of thatched roofs in the village hiding under the giant ancient tree.

Sol pictured the boat's owners playing cards in the bar, giving up the day, happier to complain about the loss than fight it.

'This one might just sail on past, like the others,' Sol said, as he helped haul the boat.

'It might,' Jacobo allowed.

Sol heard the grunt of a sore back, saw the softness in the body, the belly straining at the shirt. Jacobo was a big man but moving toward doughy.

'No point in taking any chances. Can't fish without a boat. Young man or old,' he said, letting Sol know he hadn't missed the demonstration of young strength. He was the same age as Sol's father.

A musical whistle from Agatha that mimicked a foolish-looking night bird drew their attention. Sol had grown up hearing it and realised that sometimes it hadn't been the bird at all. Agatha's daughter, Ceecee, a curly haired child playing with two boys further along the sand, looked up at the sound but ran to her father, not her mother.

'Just a little longer,' she asked. Her wide-eyed efforts to play on his affection so transparent they were irresistible.

'If the wind picks up. If it rains,' he said.

'If the tide comes in, if the waves go higher than my knee,' Ceecee continued, singsonging the words. With a triumphant grin for her mother and a wave for Sol, she ran back to her friends.

Sol waved back, then doffed an imaginary cap to Agatha. The tall woman nodded but was looking across the cove to her sister's house. The figure moving around the house must have been Rosa, with her black clothes and white hair but if she saw them, she gave no sign.

Sol examined the widow's house as he walked back to Illy. It stood alone, unprotected by the trees. The day she lost her husband, Sol's father had been on the boat, clinging to it when it washed ashore, alive but lost. He refused to set foot on a boat again. A fisherman who wouldn't fish. A husband who couldn't provide. A father who left. Now he worked for a man who bought and sold fish in another town.

The young widow had screamed at nine-year-old Sol in her swirling grief, howling at his father through him for not saving her husband, for not being the one who drowned.

Illy had calmed her. Calmed him. Illy's own father may have been a fisherman, no one knew. A ghost in the night his mother claimed till the day she died. Sol's mother said that might not be the whole story. That was as close as she came to calling anyone a liar.

'Too big to fish?' Sol asked Illy, pointing at the storm.

'Don't start that again.'

'I'm not starting anything. Just thinking we could show those old men how it's done? What do you say, my timid little friend?'

Illy took a final a sip of his beer, waiting for a grumble of thunder to roll over the tiny beach, miles from the big fight.

'Fish will have dropped low,' he said, which was neither yes nor no.

Sol grinned. He could work with that.

The Whistle

A whistle stolen from a nightbird flew across the bay. The secret signal between sisters. Three notes that made us allies.

In the spaces between them, I realised the message was for her daughter, not me. The wind fruit I'd collected in the storm fell from my hands.

In the decade since Agatha last called me, I passed from girl to widow.

In the time it took the fruit to land with a thud of flesh, I was both.

Handsome

'Do you think he knows he's handsome?' I asked Agatha, that lifetime ago.

Out of range of our mother's call, we watched Matteo spread nets to dry in the sun. He was older than us, a man, and from somewhere else.

Agatha yelped before she had a chance to answer, her face covered by two cold hands. 'You stink of fish,' she said to Jacobo, the owner of the hands, but smiled as she let him slide his arms around her.

I'd seen my big sister practice a look in our room at night that hinted she knew things she might be persuaded to teach an innocent like Jacobo. I wasn't sure what she knew, but it was more than me.

'We're going for a walk past the mangroves,' Agatha said, smoothing her skirt as she stood.

She glanced at Matteo, then fussed with my hair for a moment. 'Yes,' she said, 'I think he does.' She left me sitting on the pier that will be washed away by the same wave that takes him.

Leaf

I didn't see him look at me though I sensed it as I folded a leaf in ways nature never imagined. While my hands were busy, my thoughts were like the butterfly that came to investigate what I was doing, then spiralled on a pathway of its own.

Why was this the man I wanted to talk to me? There were others I would have silenced with a wish. Why couldn't I talk to him? I was no mouse. I wanted him to come to me. He had a fine voice. Deep and musical, with a laugh that boomed, then lingered through the trees.

Sometimes he slept on the beach, spurring delicious sleepless nights as my mind, not my body, slipped from the room I shared with my sister. My imagination crept to this unguarded treasure, sliding under the upturned boat where he lay, his bare skin against my covered body. After that things became vague, my curiosity outstripping my experience.

Agatha was on her way to marrying and having little babies in a little house. Before the same happened to me, I wanted a man to bring me the world, tell me stories of life off this island, or better still, show me. Was this him? The idea this was the moment my life began made me tingle.

It was time to let Matteo know I felt his eyes on me. I looked up, as I'd seen Agatha practice in the mirror. Let him see me, as a woman, not a girl.

He was gone. Where? Slumped somewhere in the shade? Or at the bar like the old fishermen?

I'd been trying to decide if my leaf should be a boat or a box. Now I just wanted to rip it apart.

Gift

The sun dimmed over me. Bright cold raindrops fell from the blue sky.

When I looked up, the cloud dripping the sea on to me was Matteo. A dark shape lit from behind, the glint of his smile thrilled me. He'd slipped to the other side of the pier and hauled himself out, all without my hearing or seeing.

I had been wishing for him to as I distracted myself weaving a leaf. That was strong magic.

He dropped into a crouch and locked my eyes to his. I breathed the cooling air around him. He brought his own weather. Not asking my permission, not speaking, he touched the construction in my hand and the skin that held it.

I shivered, so close I saw every drop drying on his skin, the bead at the tip of his long eyelash as he searched my eyes. He dropped something into the leaf and closed my fingers around it, not letting me look away from him. His fist dwarfed mine.

'A pearl is a secret. A gift from me to you,' he said, in that accent from nowhere, and stood. I watched every step away, aware of his body in each movement, and mine. I outlined his footprint on the wood with my finger as it dried.

Only when he grabbed the boat did I look away and watch my palm open. There, in the trembling leaf, was a pearl.

I stared at it until the long, sad three-note whistle from my sister signalled to come home. I answered with the same whistle though my lips were dry. I feared the sound wouldn't reach Agatha, as far away then as she is now, decades later.

Gamblers

On the day his parents left, Sol tied himself to the highest branch of the tree in the middle of the village and wouldn't come down until they either stayed or left without him. They left. From his perch Sol looked across the village, seeing it as he never had before. He vowed never to run away from anything.

Today the village was still an apology of huts, but it could grow. The cove was a treasure waiting for plucking. Fix the road, rebuild the pier, Sol had ideas.

The tang of the sea was sharper with every breath as he and Illy rowed to steal from the storm. The others cowered at home, so every fish was theirs. Stay for an hour, maybe less. It was a convincing plan if he ignored the towering clouds, both more solid and fluid as they got closer.

'Here,' Sol called, though it wasn't as far from shore as he wanted.

Twenty minutes later Sol wrapped the faded orange line around his wrist, wet from the previous cast, heavy from being soaked in rough sea. That had only netted a handful. Not enough to need Illy's help to haul in, and a one-man catch was not a catch at all, the old fishermen said.

He pulled the guideline tight as he grabbed the mouth of the net in his other hand. Illy cleared the lead weights at the other end, straightening the net, checking for non-existent tangles. They had been fishing for longer than they could remember, with invisible habits.

The salt and metal taste of the lead weight was familiar as Sol got a solid footing to put all his strength into the cast. As he waited for him and the boat to be in harmony, Sol didn't like the glances his friend threw at the sky. Each silent movement, even the silence itself, was a question pitched at Sol. Both knew it. Was this a fool's run, with more risk than fish to show?

Sol twisted his weight from his back foot to his front, casting the net high away from him, watching it open above the churning sea into a ring. Each lead weight stretched for freedom in a different direction.

He lost any splash on the rough surface. Only the orange thread said the net existed. Sol read the messages passed along that line in tugs and pulses. What was a current, what might be jellyfish, seaweed or driftwood? He could feel Illy read his face. Only how hard it was to haul the net clear of the water would answer this guesswork.

The rope tugged with satisfying strength, but this sea was deceptive. For all his optimism, Sol could feel the arm being drawn back for a sucker punch.

The tied mouth of the net broke the surface as Sol hauled it in, closing the bag. They had what they had, a little or a lot, or nothing at all.

A wrench in his shoulder told Sol there was weight. A flash of silver sent a tingle through him. They had a catch. He jerked his head for Illy to help.

With skill so practised it wasn't clear which hand belonged to which body they pulled it to the side, then a yank over the bucket end and released the neck so the catch skittered with a satisfying splash.

Illy leaned back, arms spread like they were having a sunset beer. 'Your highness,' he said, and cracked the lazy smile Sol had seen make grown women giggle like schoolgirls.

'Never a doubt,' he answered. They didn't fight, these two boys, grown to men, but sometimes fell out of line with each other in ways no one else would recognise. Small hesitancies, absences more than actions.

The ritual of clearing the nets and casting again took on an eager rhythm. The powerful lure of one more catch. Soon the boat was low in choppy water, more laden than it had ever been.

Illy looked to the horizon, which was closer than either had noticed.

'Home?' he said, hauling the net to join the rest of the catch.

'One more cast,' Sol answered, clearing the lines. He heard Illy's pause but carried on as if he hadn't. Bringing anything back was a victory. Bringing a boatful in the face of a storm made a legend.

'This is pushing it,' Illy said.

'So let's push it.'

They worked fast while hard needles of rain pricked them. Once it was landed they threw the catch, nets and all to the bucket end.

Wind, solid as a tree, cracked against them, sending Sol sprawling. He scrambled to his oar, skidding on entrails and fish. Whiteheads leapt the gunwale. The storm was moving.

Old Jacobo was right. But wrong too. The haul at the back of the boat was proof. Sol and Illy grinned as they rowed. They left as boys who dared the big storm, returned as the men who fished it. They just had to get the catch home.

Sol needed strength, and he knew where to look for it: in the faces of the men who had sniggered at his father, who had made sly comments, then patted the man on his back.

'That day, up the tree,' Sol said, timing his words between strokes. 'This is what I could see.' The prow dipped into the water. 'Not my father leaving.' Then rose. 'But us coming home.' A wave, higher than any other, lifted them. 'You and me.' They were flying. 'Fishing the storm.' Outrunning the wind. 'Winning.' The oars had no water to pummel. I miss him. I miss them.

They could see the tree. Knew the village was hiding below. 'Today, my friend,' Sol said as they dropped, grinning, 'we won.'

How a Widow Survives

When Matteo drowned, the air around me grew thin. I was unmoored, not even thirty and my hair turned white. Every day I walked the beach, my eyes on the borderline of the tide that had taken him, watching for another memory. They were easy to see when they were there, but most days I found nothing. Cleaning them was an offering, one of many that brought him near.

People told me time would ease my pain, and they were right. They meant Matteo would fade, but they were wrong.

He grew clearer. I saw glimpses through the window, or as I walked from the village, or when someone made a gesture that conjured him, a sound that was his, caught the light in a certain way.

You must let him go, they said, a little each day. But how? And why?

Agatha and I couldn't be in the same room. I was the wound that refused to scar. I scared off the village, but they tolerate me now. I exhausted my sister into silence.

Matteo had left me for the sea, broken his promise to return each night.

'I'll be here when you come,' I said to the bowl where I keep the stones of memory cool, until one day they won't burn. That was the other side of the promise, my part. For him to come home to me, I must be here.

On good days it helped to think like that. On bad days nothing helped. That's how a widow survives.

The-Man-Who-Did-Nothing

A long time ago, the son of the-man-who-did-nothing watched as I searched the beach for memories disguised as stones in a sea of stones. When I couldn't find Matteo, it was too painful to think. My heart knew there would be a time I would have him near, so it sent me searching for stones. Or sent them to me.

A memory can burn worse than boiling water. In the first year after my husband drowned, mine were so searing I trapped them in stones, kept them in water that vanished overnight. The once molten ancient rocks burned and boiled, then cooled, then burned and boiled again. One day I hoped to open them, extract the memories when they cooled, or when my skin hardened.

They called me widow. I lost my name along with my roles as sister or daughter, wife, mother too I supposed, all gone from me.

I ignored them. Or tried to. The quiet friend tried to say something. I howled him away. Hadn't they been taunting me moments before?

I couldn't see them as boys. All I saw was the son of the-man-who-did-nothing to save Matteo. The man who looked at me, tears brimming in his eyes and said, 'One second he was there. The next he was gone.' As if that wasn't my story, the moment my life balanced on.

Who was he to cry? He had a wife, a child, this boy, some-one to hold him, someone to hold. 'Why didn't you reach out? Why didn't you grab him?' I said, which were all ways of howl-ing, 'Why wasn't it you?'

I screamed at the boys. Took sand and threw it at them. I thought that happened in my head, but my hands were filthy and bloodied.

When I fell to my knees, whimpering and sorry, they were too far away and circling each other, absorbed in retelling what happened, reinventing it.

That's when I hit the black stone, sharp against my knee. I stared down at it, seeing it was a memory. The best truths cut me open, so I rocked until the skin split, seeing the blood leach into the sand, kneeling heavier to cut deeper, chasing more pain.

Later I held that stone to my neck, jagged against the pulse and pressed. It was the sharpest thing in the house, though didn't cut deep as a memory. I only had seconds before I had to put it in water again. It blistered against my skin. I watched a drop of blood fall into the water. It hung suspended, a twisted tear like a memory that lost its form, diluted but ever-present under shivering water that returned to glass.

I took the stone from my throat. I was the whetstone, not the sacrifice. I heard the laughing boys. The sea had not smoothed the black stone and never would. It was jagged and sharp too, and for a long time, my favourite in its vengeful agony.

Prayers

The pearl nestled between dry stones so full of memories they burned water. I took it and rubbed it against my tooth, felt its grit. My husband told me, years before he drowned, that was how you knew a pearl was real.

When I dropped it into the second filled bowl, my reflection broke into fragments. While the water calmed, I prayed his face would join mine in the renewed mirror.

An unworthy question hid in my plea. Would I be as ripe with youth and hope as I was that blue-skyed day, or eroded by time and mourning? The water answered with my face, alone and exhausted.

For Matteo there was no question. He was preserved in the prime of death.

Skimmer

I picked a skimmer from the bowl of dry stones and pictured Matteo weighing it in an open palm, glancing at me as if waiting for my verdict.

Even a decade later, with him dead and me alone in my kitchen, I shook my head and laughed, called him a fool.

Salt whitened my fingers as I cleaned the stone, then slid it into the wet bowl, making the smallest ripple.

It was then I realised, just to play with him, I'd made it a game.

Dead, but Not Departed

The grey stone with its red stripe curled like a banner was a memory of a sultry evening sitting outside. Matteo had his back against the house, and I had my back against his chest. It was too hot to sit like that, adding body heat to the combustible air, but it tasted of defiance as the last of the sun danced blood and purple across the sea for us.

He had his arms around me as we took turns with the sweating bottle of beer. When his hand was free, he ran a chilled finger down my throat and let it linger above my chest as I swallowed.

The water splashed when I dropped the stone, and in the valleys of the ripples, I saw a flicker of my husband, dead but not departed.

The Straw Doll

'Why did you take so long?' Ceecee shivered past me to get inside. The storm was all wind and rain now; the thunder and lightning saving themselves for night.

'I was looking for something,' I said, almost telling the truth. I had been trying to call back my dead husband.

'You were staring at those bowls.' She had seen me.

'Does your mother know you're here?' I said, to deflect. I am the aunt who went crazy. The widowed sister who can't move on or let go or whatever you do when your life ends but you're still breathing. Agatha and I don't speak.

'I told Juan to tell her. She can't be mad at that. Why didn't you open the door?'

I looked for a towel.

'Who were you talking to, Auntie?'

'No one, sweety, I was alone.'

'But I saw you talking to someone. Was it your husband?'

'Husband?' The word rolled around my mouth like an ash pebble. Confetti bloomed, falling through the electric air. They tickled my skin as they floated, raining from a cloudburst of memories, never landing. Agatha and I made them the evening before my wedding, tearing blossoms into baskets. Our last night as sisters, we said. Now we would both be wives. We giggled about our first meetings with boys, stolen kisses, telling mother about the marriage; times when anything was possible.

'Auntie Rosa. Keep your eyes closed.'

I obeyed the order, not knowing I'd shut them.

'Now open,' she said.

I saw a straw doll, inches from my nose.

'I will keep you safe,' the doll said, a little girl making her voice deep. 'I made it.' Ceecee relapsed into her delicious giggle.

I made a laugh from the burning lump in my throat and took the doll from Ceecee, making a great fuss of putting it in the window where it could stare away the storm.

'There,' I said and dug my nails into my palm, searching for strength I didn't have, blindsided by a child's kindness. 'Now I won't be so alone.'

A Little Accident

'Is that a stone?' Ceecee demanded between sticky mouthfuls, pointing her fork at a blue-lit piece on my shelf.

'Not a stone,' I said. 'But close your eyes.'

Ceecee put her fork down, grinning as I reversed our game. She squeezed her eyes shut and held her arms out straight from her body.

I took the smooth blue nugget from the shelf and fought every urge to put it back before sliding it into Ceecee's hand. Every object on that shelf connected to my husband.

'It's a stone. But it's getting warm and—' she squealed.

'You peeked.'

'It's a fly,' Ceecee said, wide-mouthed, peering at the treasure in her hand. 'A fly in a stone.'

'It's blue amber.' A flicker in the light said it pleased Matteo that I shared a little of us with the child.

'Is it real?'

'Oh, yes. Thousands of years ago he got stuck in sticky stuff from a tree, trapping him.'

Ceecee held the amber up to her eye. 'Hello, Mr Fly. Sorry you got stuck inside a rock. But if you didn't, I would never have got to meet you.'

'Someone special brought it back to me,' I said, taking the treasure back and replacing it on the shelf, trying to find the spot where the light picked it out, but it had vanished. There was a break between storms. They skidded past our forgotten island, catching us with sideways glances until one turned its full attention to us.

'Time for you to go home, little miss,' I said.

Ceecee pulled a half-hearted face.

'Can I bring something from your shelf?' she asked. 'I'll be careful. I promise.' She dragged out the last word.

'No, no... everything must...' Nothing must ever leave the house; the puzzle needed all its pieces.

Her expression moved from half to broken-hearted.

'I can show you one more thing,' I said. 'But this one you can't touch. Promise?'

'Promise,' she said.

I took the glass sphere on its wooden base, surrounding an island that looked like ours, or a thousand others from the shelf and held it in front of Ceecee, seeing her face distort through it. She peered over a small green mountain with a too-big tree, a brown cottage, a flesh-coloured beach surrounded by blue sea.

'This is our home. Can you see it?'

She nodded, but she couldn't.

'Now...' I shook it and watched Ceecee's eyes widen as she saw the sky around the island fill with gold flakes that drifted from the water-filled sky. Her hands reached, but she clamped them back to her sides.

'It's like treasure,' she said. 'Shake it again.'

'I'll throw all the gold up in the air, and you bring it back.' I shook the globe near Ceecee's eyes then pulled it back so it sat on the table. 'Look around the room. Can you see the gold falling?'

She looked dubious until I plucked a leaf from the air so daintily she saw it.

'I can, I can.' Ceecee staggered as if the ground was trembling then squealed as she ran around the room, grabbing imaginary leaves from the air, depositing them on my lap and racing away. 'We're rich, Auntie Rosa.'

As she dropped the next batch, I squeezed her tight. 'You're so clever. You can see what's not there.'

Ceecee giggled at the conspiracy, then spun away from me, knocking against the table, tilting the globe from its wooden cradle. Even as I grabbed for it, it rolled away and dropped over the edge, tumbling to the stone floor in a splintering splash of glass and water.

'I'm sorry, I'm sorry. I didn't mean it. It was an accident. I'm sorry.' Ceecee looked at my face, then shrieked as I swooped.

I lifted her to the doorway. 'Your feet. Glass,' I said as if that was the reason. 'Go. I'll clean it up. Don't cry. Go before the storm. It will be fine...' I lied and closed the door on tears that would soon dry, and then knelt on broken glass I could never put back together.

No Horizon

However hard Sol and Illy rowed, the village never got closer. There was only storm and sea. The sky had fled, and they clung to their oars like prayers. The sea had teeth. The thudding rain against the wood drew splinters.

Illy was ashen with cold, exhaustion and fear. Only instinct forced Sol to row, though his body convulsed. He had no breath to speak. Every pull made him want to throw up, but they were covering no distance. If they stopped they were lost, but they couldn't continue.

The boat lurched and wrenched the oar from Sol's hand. He scrambled to grab it back, but the deck fell away as the thin boat, a twig in this sea, snapped vertical. For an insane instant Illy was suspended above Sol's head, and the world pivoted around him.

It rained dead fish as the catch dropped and both men fell, wrapped in each other. Even in the tumult Sol felt Illy's head slam against the water as if he'd hit stone. The impact exploded any air from Sol's lungs, and his ears rang. He tasted blood.

They fell, if falling was the word. Sometimes in air, sometimes water. Sol breathed when he could, instinct deciding, thought too slow. He clung to Illy, who didn't cling back.

Invisible currents churned and twisted. Sol kicked as best he could toward what he hoped was the surface, where the waves were thirty feet tall, then toward what he hoped was the shore. He would not give up. Could not. There was no way to tell if they were moving closer or moving at all, but he kicked out against the sea because it was all he knew to do. Kicked again. And again.

A tug on his leg wrenched, but he ignored it. It came again, gripping him harder. Sol lashed out with both feet, hoping to strike a tender spot on whatever had him. His foot found another mouth and thrashed, from primal terror, and to stay afloat.

Sol searched for a shape, a flash of colour or skin at his feet, then realised it was his own fishing net, weighted and twisted around him.

What small relief there was drowned in panicked despair. The tangled net dragged them both under and kept them there. He stopped kicking. Every movement tightened the mess around his legs. Nothing would give, and they fell, deeper.

To untangle them, he would have to let go of Illy. If he did that he might never find him again. If he didn't let go, they could both drown. Sol saw the bubbles of his breath rise away, leaving him trapped in that impossible moment.

The Wave

When I looked out the window, my dead husband waved from the unquiet beach. I thought I'd never see him again, so I waved back. He looked at a tree upended by the storm. Its leaves and roots flapped in the high wind though not a hair stirred on his head. I'd guided Matteo back with precise rituals and curated memories. Sometimes he sat with me, drinking tea, while I talked about the simple things of the day, but he'd never acknowledged me, until now.

I took instruction from a ghost, not knowing if horror or happiness was waiting. The squall was rising again, but I stepped from my home and across the debris of its first assault, through the restless shifting of loose branches and long fronds, torn nets and crab carcasses.

Matteo stared at the churned sand by his feet, and with a lurch, I thought of Ceecee. I'd sent my niece along this path but hadn't tracked her to the village. She was easily distracted.

I looked where he looked. Chaos churned the earth with dirt, sand, leaf, root, branch, bone, skin, face, leg, blood, teeth, gristle, entrails. It wasn't Ceecee.

The stench brought a heave from my stomach and a slime of cold sweat. An arm twisted against a body at an impossible angle. There were too many feet and hands in the puzzle, but there was only one head. It had a deep gash across a staring eye and white flecks of broken bone, too bright against clotting blood not pumped by any living heart. Spasms lurched in an irregular pulse. I looked at the outrage and felt the weakness of gravity.

This ruination clawed its way from the underworld with one of three hands while the eyes on what remained of the face, cheek ripped open and a flap of skin raw with matted hair, stared at the lifeless sky above me.

Was this something to help or flee from?

The puzzle shifted. Another face emerged from under the broken one. One man trapped under another. Those glazed eyes looked around, not picking me out from the sky or the trees, but I had seen and been seen.

Voices came from the road.

My drowned husband had led me to this, but he fled, his spectral presence no match for fresh stinking death.

There was no beauty in this, no poetry, no hope.

I ran from the voices on the road and twisted bodies on the beach, toward home, praying mortality's more welcome face waited for me, that my husband, ghostly and unscarred, would be there.

The wind searched for a way to knock me. Each rock and branch tripped and slapped me. I crashed over a rust-encrusted metal bar. Drunk from pain, I used it to lever myself upright, then as a cane to get me home.

The house was empty. There was no life, and worse, no death. My long-drowned husband had shown me raw death, then left me to choke on it alone.

I forced myself to look through the window at the men from the village, other men in their arms, my niece Ceecee leading the grim parade. The bodies were Sol and Illy. They'd been on the beach this morning. When I made tea for my dead husband, I'd seen them through this window.

The swell rolled over me, the great tides fought for control, my pain and grief, this new horror. Sol's father had been on the boat when Matteo drowned. My cry strangled as shame erupted for setting tragedy in competition. I gripped the inside of the window, hearing my breathing catch in my chest. Agony flared inside me like a fire, relighting my loss while smouldering grief burned my eyes.

A straw doll Ceecee had brought me filled my vision, an innocent gift, trying to help. As I stared, it grew larger than the window, stronger than storms. I clung to it.

On the Beach, Lying

Sol felt sand under his fingers and air between his lips, not water. Breathing was exhausting though he was no longer at sea. There was a pressure on his chest. Around him the storm rumbled on, but something sheltered him. His thoughts had the same slip-sand quality as the coast between the sea of sleep and the dry land of waking. He kept his eyes closed.

As a child there had been dreams where he couldn't move a muscle, however hard he tried. Then feared moving when he woke, in case he couldn't.

Sol didn't want to open his eyes. He remembered, dreamed, imagined that he had opened them already and seen the widow watching over him. But that made no sense. He had seen something else too.

Why was it so hard to breathe?

He was that boy again, paralysed by a dream. The house was quiet around him. His father was already fishing, and his mother moving with her restrained efficiency. It was the fear of not being able to move that kept his eyes closed then. Now it was fear of what he might see that sealed them. But he had to look, he was a man now and had to fight fears.

Sol opened his eyes.

There was no widow, only racing dark clouds and shaking trees. The howling told him the wind was blasting, but he couldn't feel it on his skin. His friend Illy, lying above him, protected him, even in death.

Sol closed his eyes. Didn't move.

The Trunk

I sat in front of the locked trunk while the storm blustered outside like a fat drunk. An iron bar lay on my bedroom floor, between me and that lock.

Every day in the first year after my husband died, I'd wanted to open the trunk. To get closer to whatever secrets he kept in there. But I didn't. Not through pride or respect, but because it burned too hot. My nerves were so raw I struggled to touch the black wood of the chest, never mind the lock, never mind force it open.

Later, with Matteo near again, I didn't need it as much, and he would see if I broke it open. More than that, it might stop him coming back.

I had lost Matteo. Just like the first year. A howling void worse than any storm.

Every day he took the key with him, even on the day he never came back. That was for a reason. But why should we have secrets, then or now? We were husband and wife; we were lovers. I recoiled from the thought I had been a widow longer than a wife but used it to lift the bar and slot it into the circle that held the lock.

With my foot against the chest, I leaned back, worried about scoring the old wood as I levered against it, but it didn't take long before I didn't care. I needed to see what was inside this box I struggled to slide, much less lift. My heart raced from the exertion of forcing the old rusted lock and the fearful excitement of what I would find.

I had never seen Matteo put anything in there or take anything out though the key creaked and the lid moaned when he lifted it, alone in the room. When I asked what was in it, he would tease me with wouldn't you like to know and oh, nothing at all.

One night, rumdrunk from Hector's bar, he answered, saying, 'That trunk is me. I am that trunk,' but turned it into, 'I am that drunk,' and I allowed myself to be distracted.

Something cracked. The lock was unbroken but the metal panel it attached to gave way. I fell back, slamming my hip against the bed and sat looking at the trunk I didn't want to open. Now it was free, I wanted the lock back in place.

I had spent hours looking at it, wondering what secrets he kept hidden from me in there. How wrong it was for me to look, how foolish to not? I had wanted clues to who he was, to understand him, but now I just wanted there to be a trace of him.

I lifted the lid before I lost my nerve and saw that Matteo had been telling the truth. The chest, for all its weight, was empty.

Several Uses for Music

I turned the handle on the record player twenty times, the number remembered from when Agatha and I would play the same three records over and over as girls. The player was old even then, and the records we played are long gone. But the rule was twenty times. Enough to get to the end of the song but not so much to overwind the spring.

We danced and chased each other round the room until our mother told us to shut up or she would take that damned thing away.

I placed the heavy needle on the circling record, and the simple bass notes played, the repeated piano melody, then the violins, so wise and slow. This was a record Matteo brought me. A kind of music I'd never heard. The same instruments made it as the old boring stuff we made fun of, but it didn't sound old. It was for dancing and grown-ups, and love and seduction and now I knew, for loss.

Silent Notes

As the music played, and dangerous feelings welled in my chest, I took a pen Matteo gave me and wrote.

One night, when it was too hot to sleep and too beautiful to stay inside, a man and a woman danced on the beach. Music came in from the sea, and it was the most beautiful sound either of them had heard.

The night played the music on the sea. Each piano note picked out in silver by the moon, each long wave rising, stretching and breaking was the violin, and the sea itself, unseen and all-powerful in the darkness was the bass of hidden currents.

The man and woman turned and swayed, even as the tide came in. Each movement was an answer to a question, and each return a promise. The music entwined them and enchanted them while the tide rose higher. And still they danced.

He held her in his strong arms, and she lay her head against his chest. They murmured to each other in voices lower than the sea, quieter than the music only they heard.

And when the waves rose so high around them, they couldn't speak, first her, then him, they continued to dance, content to hold and be held.

Their steps never faltered, and the music never quietened as they danced at the bottom of the sea. If one needed air, then the other kissed them and then returned the breath when the time came. Above them, far above them, the moon dropped sil-

ver notes on to the placid surface, and these notes fell by their feet as they danced.

The tide went out, and the shush of the waves returned but didn't drown the music as the water dropped to her ankles again, and she was dancing on the beach, but it was daylight now, and she was dancing on her own, and she couldn't stop, was afraid to stop, and didn't know how, and the music was so beautiful, and she had been the happiest she had ever been, and to lose the music would have been agony.

So she kept dancing, and people say that on a night when the moon drips silver on the sea, you can see her, and if you listen hard, you can hear music.

They come to see this woman, dancing on the sand, turning to music just out of reach and though some of them suspect it is the most beautiful music in the world, they can't hear it.

I had that melody in my head when I put down the pen, though I couldn't sing it since it was composed of notes only in my mind.

Click, Click, Click

The record wound down. When the needle click, click, clicked against the final groove, getting slower and slower as the spring weakened, I lifted it and put it back in its cradle and cracked the vinyl in half against the table.

The rituals that guided my husband back had failed me, and I had to find new ones.

I took the piece of paper I'd written on and held it close to the candle flame though not quite touching. I could only do so much, and that was more than I could bear. It would catch fire, or it would not. The hope brought a sob, and that sob shuddered the paper and flame close enough to marry.

The agony of losing Matteo burned me as I watched the paper he'd brought me curl, and my words of us with it. Even the flame biting my fingers was not as painful, but in the end I had to let go since there was nothing left to hold.

Listening Now

'He's down. He's down. There's no coming back from this.'

Sol swam through darkness, heart thundering as he flailed awake. There was a chair beside his bed, with a glass of water on it.

He tried to sustain the thought he was asleep. If nothing had happened, nobody would be sitting watch. He wouldn't be here to be watched. The crack in the wish let through the truth.

'The Kid has taken a battering.'

The radio. Someone must have turned on the radio. A boxing match.

He moved, and every bone and muscle lit up in pain, stunning him back to helpless stillness. Each painful breath was a reminder he was trapped under the fact of Illy—

He had been on the beach. In the storm. With Illy who was— No. Think straight.

'He's getting up.'

Sol threw himself from the bed and roared to block the pain and memory. As he stood, the sweat on his body cooled. He spat up a stream of liquid so vile and sudden it left him gasping. He swayed above it, fists clenching and unclenching.

'The kid is reeling. The kid is reeling.'

Sol grabbed the chair and attacked the radio. Smashed and pummelled the thing that just jumped around under assault.

A chair leg cracked like a bone, and the seat flew with a clatter across the floor. He threw the radio against a wall, roaring when it smashed, spewing plastic and parts.

'The Kid is down.'

Sol stared at the radio, broken beyond any chance of life. Then he saw the magazines, those boxing books that his father let him read as a boy. Blow by blow accounts of the great fights, interviews with the champions, speculation about upcoming fights that were now history. And those photos. Images of champions, gods, who could take any pain and still prevail. These were men. They did what they had to. They endured.

Sol swiped at the pages with the stick he had reduced the chair to, revelling in the ripped paper, concentrating hard on destruction even as his arms burned. Panting, he stood over an image, his favourite. The greatest champion, over a prostrate opponent, taunting him even as the referee, puny beside this deity, holds him back. But trickery blurred and faded the champion until all Sol could see was the fallen boxer, unconscious on the mat. In every fight there was a loser.

There was nothing left to break in here, but outside this room there was them, with their judgement and accusation, their hypocrisy, lies, petty rules and rituals, the excuses for tiny lives on this rock in the middle of the ocean, year after year. He felt their eyes on him, and his chest rose, muscles tightening. What had they done to save Illy? Nothing. The opposite of nothing.

Beyond them was the storm that could rip them all apart or pass by, meaningless and cruel, destructive for the sake of it.

In here were Sol's thoughts, and that made the choice.

Sol tore into the living room, blasting through the door, kicking at everything, not looking at the table in the living room's centre. He broke every cup and plate, every chair, ripped a painting apart, a curtain from the window. He punched the wall, not seeing the blood mark he left, before he kicked at the armchair where Illy used to sit, picking out notes of old songs, or meandering through ones of his own.

The guitar stood nestled in the corner. Sol picked it up by the neck, panting out of all proportion to the physical exertion. His fingers ached to unpick the frets, to tear the strings away, to smash the body against the wall but his muscles locked.

His body stood at war with itself, a battle that teetered until, more slowly than he had ever moved, Sol placed the guitar back in its place. The process took minutes, and for all of them it terrified Sol. That any harm could come to the guitar had cold sweat running down his back. He had to protect it at all costs. It was the most precious, fragile thing in the world and even breathing hard while it was in his care might destroy it. As it touched the ground, the bass string hummed and Sol whimpered to hear it was a pure note. He had not hurt it; he had not disappointed it.

The journey back to Illy on the table took almost as long as laying down the guitar. Once there, he lay his hand on his friend's silent chest.

'I'm listening now,' he said, his voice like a child.

Found, and Lost

The storm inhaled, preparing to roar again. My sister was at my door, her daughter tangled at her waist. Agatha hadn't spoken to me in years, and now I didn't understand the words she said. They won't stay in my head long enough to join into meaning. Time has broken down. A tree in the village fell, she said. I may have heard either the fall or word of it. Her husband is hurt, and something damaged their house. Could Ceecee stay with me? She tells me about the boy the storm took, but I knew that. I saw the body, twisted. Found it. Him.

'...her to be with you, in the storm?' I heard and I nod hello.

She left, and Ceecee shouted questions in my house. I will ask Agatha in. Does she need to stay too? I don't hate her. She hates me. But she went.

They kissed and hugged, mother and daughter. Before or after Agatha lifted her hand toward my arm. Her reality takes too long to reach me, for me to respond.

By the time I thought to say it is good to be close enough to see your few grey hairs, so good, she was gone.

The Straw Man

The winds snapped to life again, and I was a kite in a storm held by a frayed string in the hands of a child. I didn't know why my sister left her daughter in my house. A message, an apology, a test, worry bead, protection, in pity, in desperation?

'What's this for?' she said, looking at my kitchen floor, covered in straw I had been saving to thatch the roof. That was a good question. Rituals I'd never believed in had worked but were now lost, broken by accidents, both little and tragic. I needed to rebelieve in new forms, but it's hard to plan faith.

'I want to make something,' I said. 'And you can help me.'

'But what is it?'

'Something to protect us. Someone,' I said, the reasons coming to life as I spoke. 'It was your idea. You gave me a little doll, now we'll make a big one, big as a man.' I hoped my terror sounded like excitement, my desperation like the start of an adventure.

'Make straight bunches,' I said, showing with lengths of tough straw, tying them off with softer strands.

Ceecee did as instructed. 'Easy,' she said, presenting it.

'That's good,' I said, feeding on the excited gleam in her eye. 'Now let's do lot's more.'

At first I selected the pieces but soon she was picking her own. While she continued, sitting in the fleeting dark and skittering light of the growing storm outside, I took batches away and laid them out to one side. When Ceecee returned from the world of her own creation, selection and production, she stood, tilting her head this way and that until she realised what she was seeing.

The proportions of the body were of a man, built around the spine of a long metal bar, the head shaped with eyes and a mouth, arms held out like a cross, legs strong enough to stand.

I told her I was planning to pin it above the front door. Hang it on the anchor my husband had put there years ago. 'I don't believe in all of that,' I said, petrified to be silent now I had thrown words like wild seeds. They fell like they hadn't for years, with no thought to their danger, their implications. 'I don't. You need a strong mind. But an open mind too. How will we learn otherwise? How? Listen. Think.'

Ceecee had no idea what I was talking about.

'Bad things have happened, Ceecee,' I said, and she understood that. As we worked, she talked to me about a tree that fell and the man they found on the beach, and how the tree broke her room, and her father now walked like an old woman.

Her chatter tugged me back to earth with each concern and story, each wide-eyed opening to the disasters of this world, seen for the first time through her eyes.

We finished the straw man and eased it upright. I held it around the waist with one hand, cradling its head with the other. Ceecee burst into giggles. 'You're dancing.'

She was right, though it was a dance of echoes of other dances, with stronger arms around me where I didn't have to lead, alone.

'Open the door, I said. Ceecee laboured in gusts grown bold in the hours we'd been working. 'And now the chair,' I said.

The brewing storm watched us, undecided if we were feeding or defying it.

'Hold it steady,' I said, stepping on to the chair.

Ceecee had the serious look of a child on important grown-up business. The straw man stood by her, invigorated by the wind.

I took the wreath from the anchor above my door, a memento of my husband even I failed to preserve. The dry leaves crackled and broke as I handed them down, whipped by the breeze.

Ceecee spluttered and coughed so hard I had to reach to steady the man, struggling for balance of my own. I crouched, eye level with my niece as she shook the remains of the wreath from her hair.

The straw man was heavy as I hooked him to the anchor by the iron spar, but the wind helped me lift him. From there he had the highest view of all across the bay, over the village and to the sea.

'He can keep us safe,' I called out to Ceecee, as if that was his main job. I didn't say his true purpose was to guide my husband home from the sea that had taken him before this child was born.

When she held her hand up for me, I hesitated before I took it, not sure this kite was ready to come back to earth.

Taking the Body

The wind searched the sheet in Sol's arms, trying to steal the body inside. Another barrage of thunder and lightning approached from the sea, growing louder and closer. He was aware of being barefoot, of a door slamming behind him, but he clung to the shattered body of his childhood friend as his only certainty.

Sol wanted to take Illy to the beach. There might be a chance, a deal he could make. Something he could do, even if he didn't know what, as long as he could get him away from these people. The widow was there. She knew things and might help.

The storm tilted the village at a sickening angle as he walked, forcing him to stop every few steps. The enormous tree leaned partway between standing and falling, half its roots in the air, the rest clinging to the earth. It groaned in response to the wind, defiant but losing. There were no lights from any of the houses, and no roofs on some.

Sol's arms and shoulders, his legs and back, burned from the exertion of the day and the night, and he welcomed the pain. The more he offered, the better.

He took an hour to reach the crest of the beach in these agonising shuffles, and there he lost balance, slamming to his knees with a wet slap, Illy falling from him. When he tried to lift him again, his arms couldn't do it.

He stood and dragged the bloodied sheet with the broken body across the sand, keeping his eyes on the light in the widow's house, roaring at the wind, the sea, the sky, the lightning, but the storm grew louder to let him know he was nothing, tiny.

Worse, the sea looked so far away, even though it was further up the beach than it had any right to be. To taunt him, lightning electrified the water, changed the consistency of the air. There was no rain, but his skin prickled.

It brought back a memory of Illy telling him not to be the tallest thing around in a lightning storm. He also remembered what he had done in response to that. Run on to the beach daring the lightning to strike him.

Back then he didn't believe it would ever hit him; now he didn't care.

The Smuggler

The house vibrated in time with the slamming waves. The never-ending roar of the sea let me know it hadn't forgotten me, backed by a cacophony of crashes, shudders and growls as boats unmoored, trees bent, and plants uprooted.

Ceecee slept in my room, better than I had for years. I had hung protection over my front door, a straw man to keep away the storm that prowled the island, and to call the ghost of my husband back.

I saw a luminous form on the screaming beach, and I stepped into the night, my eyes locked on his shape, terrified to lose it in the inconstant light. A vein of lightning pulsed over the sea, seizing the rushing clouds. The figure on the sand fell to his knees, laying down what he carried. My mind twisted to make it Matteo and failed. I had seen him because I wanted to see him. What other fool was out in this weather and not already dead?

I took another step, but the wind suspended me. I'd have to fight to go forward. It was a strain to stay in place, but if I didn't, I would tumble, and if I lost my footing on the earth tonight, I might never regain it.

In front of me, the figure I wanted to be Matteo was the boy Sol. The thing he no longer carried was the body of his friend, Illy. The thunder reminded me I'd left a sleeping child behind.

I hung in the air, my own question mark, until an answer came.

The storm took a victim. But might it also make an opportunity? It overturned everything. One body might lead to another. A storm destroys, overturns, reveals.

My compass reset, I forced my foot down in defiance. Ceecee was safe in my house, exhausted and protected.

'The poor boy,' I said, stumbling to my knees beside Sol. Every word was a shout in the chaos. My hand fell on the crude shroud that covered Illy, soaked so it outlined his frame.

'You cursed him,' Sol said. The words were an accusation, but his face was a plea.

'Cursed?' I had no memory of that.

'They say you can see them. Talk to them,' he said, and I got a sense of what he wanted from me. A swirling tangle of branches pinwheeled past, tearing warnings in the wet sand.

'I need you to tell him something. From me.'

'I can try,' I said. I was brazen, I was cruel, I was in pain, I had no such power. If I made wishes come true, I wouldn't be a widow on a windswept beach taking advantage of a young man's grief.

'What do you want to tell him?'

'That I'm sorry.'

'That's not all?' I said, stalling for time. I needed to find the dead man's hand. 'He knows that. That's what we all want to say when they're gone.'

'I miss him so much already.'

I tried to speak, but an ache in my chest stopped me.

'Damn you,' he said, and I hung my head, but he wasn't talking to me. 'This is useless.'

'Keep trying,' I said, transferring the pearl from my skirt. It was the first thing Matteo gave me, and my last desperate offering.

'I think you knew, and I wanted to tell you. You are my friend. Were my...' He ground his jaw.

I squeezed the dead boy's hand around the pearl. 'Now lay him to rest in the sea.' I was shameless.

As Sol stood, I whispered to the face outlined by the heavy cloth. 'Take this to him. Tell him I love him. Tell him to come to me.'

It was a gift poisoned by cruelty, selfishness and deceit. I craved compassion and showed none. Wanted a miracle, so faked one. Saw a storm as a plough and planted a lie. I didn't care that I'd deluded one and made a messenger of another. The greed of grief is boundless, my pain so real it granted me exemption from humanity.

Fire

I sat in the filthy sand and watched the grieving man I'd lied to stagger to the ravenous sea, the corpse of his best friend in his arms. Lightning hit my house with the biblical morality of a dream, but the crack of it in my chest and the chiming deafness, was real.

A straw man hung above my door like a ward of protection. Really it was a lure to charm my dead husband back. But it, like my other delusions and lies, drew lightning.

The straw man shattered into a dozen flaming pieces, toyed with then swallowed by the wind. The roof my niece slept under jumped, and the thatch burst into golden light, fanned by a gale for once not needled with rain.

This was where I should wake from a nightmare, but I wasn't asleep.

I ran toward my burning house, knowing Ceecee's bewildered terror, woken by the loudest truest thing she'd ever heard.

Sol ran ahead of me, desperate to clear his conscience through mindless heroism. He had no jabs of his own to throw but refused to fall. From how hard he pushed through the gale, he'd already burst into the house and rescued the child; and so was forgiven by the body on the beach. I knew a little about delusion.

Every movement was too slow as we took punch after punch from gust after gust. Ahead of us the window I spent years staring through, looking for my beloved ghost, danced with uncanny beauty. Then exploded. Sol staggered back on to me, a pincushion of blinded agony while, trapped under him, I watched my world burn.

Where My Life Ended, Again

I whistled into the howling night. The bird call, once a secret signal between my sister and me, wouldn't reach her through the storm, nor could she know what it meant, but I had to confess what I'd done. I'd left her child in a burning building.

I clawed at the smouldering door, skin raw, eyes streaming, lungs tearing, achieving nothing. The fire trapped Ceecee inside; Sol flailed part-blind behind me, both helpless against my madness.

Not all cries are heard, but mine was. Or a mother's heart grasped her child's terror. Other hands joined me, my sister's hands. The door buckled and broke under our assault but wedged against an orange veined beam. There was no pushing past it though we tried beyond all sense.

I grabbed Agatha, so much the woman to my small frame, and pulled her round the side of the house. There might be another way. Heat charred terror made every thought and action torture, but I pointed to the porthole Matteo and I had cut into our roof to look at the stars when we were first married, and he was alive.

'Lift me,' I said, and she let herself be told. I scuttled up the wall like a rat and smashed the porthole open as I pinwheeled through in a tumble of arms and legs.

'The bed is empty,' I retched through fumes.

Agatha shouted, 'Under. She would hide under.'

I threw myself to the blistered floor, searching the space under the bed.

'Is she there?' Agatha asked. 'Can you see her?' The singing despair and terror in her voice would have choked me if the smoke hadn't done it already. Sol mumbled beside her as he dragged himself back into the battle.

'Shut up,' I said.

'I can't hear. I don't understand.'

'Listen.'

'What?'

'Shhhh...' I said.

Burning air filled the breath of fire with the crack and snap of everything it touched. Cloth curled, fell with a thump, timber warped and screeched as it twisted out of shape. Glass shattered, cups fell and broke.

And there it was again. A cough. Not the cracked hacking of an adult but a small shallow cough. Where?

I crawled to the door, trying not to make more noise than my rasping breath. The treacherous smoke pinned me to the ground; the door was scorching to touch. In this game of hide and seek every breath left a scar on my lungs, every movement cost me half my remaining strength, every second's cost to Ceecee might be fatal.

The cough again.

I twisted. Saw Matteo's trunk. Scrabbled to it, not daring to hope. My sweating fingers were useless over the latches, and my eyes streamed from exertion and dread. I tried to call out, but my lungs warped, and my throat rebelled. I prised open the lid of the hulking chest. Curled inside, Ceecee was too frightened to open her mouth, but as soon as she saw me, she clung to my chest and gripped with strength neither of us knew she had. In her little fist a piece of blue amber glowed in the firelight like a talisman.

I'd found her but had to do more than hold her close while we died. I looked to the porthole, wondering how to get her there in the toxic air and saw arms hang like short ropes. With me as a footstool, her little feet scampered up the smoke pillar that chimneyed out.

I collapsed onto the trunk in my blazing house, inhaling poison. My skin blistered to the touch, my home gone and every possession with it. Above me my niece's feet dangled as her mother pulled her clear, and I was happy as I waited for the end.

A furious roof beam ripped through my kitchen wall and cracked the marital bed while I cowered in the smoke. Burning potions scented the choking air, and the stones cracked open. I knelt as a blazing witness while the memories I'd stored of my husband flowed, molten and lost.

He gave me a pearl one radiant day, and my life as a daughter ended. A wave took him, and I was no longer a wife. I cried too exuberantly for him, and I had no sister. Lightning hit my house, and I was no aunt to the sleeping child I left while I searched for a chance to return the pearl.

I lay down under the smoke. This was where my life ended. Again.

Rescue

They clawed at the walls. The boy who needed to be a hero, the sister riddled with hate and guilt, the child I left to die. They were rescuing me, but I didn't want saving. Freedom was inside this pyre; escape was a prison. Bury me in the ashes of what I built.

My sister's voice called, but I had no answer. Arms reached for me. I didn't reach back. I couldn't leave my home and memories. This was where I made love to him, where I drank tea with his ghost, made an altar of his memories, collected and stored them in stones, born and now destroyed, in fire. The bellowing wind cheered the flames that ate everything and singed my eyes closed.

The house sucked a deep breath of fuel for its final inferno before it lit the night sky, saluting the retreating storm.

I saw it from outside. They had rescued me. Salvation, like damnation, can happen when you least want it.

The Last Walk

Bitter smoke defied the dying storm and followed me across the sand. I started this walk to the sea many times, and I would finish it now.

Wave after wave smashed the voracious shoreline, reaching for me through branches and stumps, dead fish and twisted nets, boat parts and glass. And a body it had perversely refused. I'd tried to smuggle the pearl to my dead husband on the corpse of another, but I retrieved it. I will return this gift in person.

The urge to look at the wreckage of my house was a knot in my back but I didn't need to see the charred walls, the wet wreckage of everything I owned, every twisted memento destroyed.

A stone tore at my sole, ripping the flesh to my heel, but I kept my eyes on the waves, relishing the sting of sand and salt, the tingle of numbness.

I was going to him. The water was up to my ankle. The sea warmer than the past in its indifference. As it pushed against me, it strengthened my stride. The tangible sting cut the bitter smoke, and the gusts that staggered me gave something to push against. The sea needs no one but accepts anyone.

My thighs ached as I waded deeper and the chill of the water slid up my body. Each breath echoed loud from tight lungs. A metal taste replaced smoke in my mouth. I wept from the fire and the thought Matteo was out there in front of me and had been all the time.

I'd fetishised my loss, nursed my grief to avoid looking at it. It became a thing in itself, an other, a set of steps to get me through each day, moving but never forward, circling, anchored.

It wasn't real, not like the slap of the sea and wind, the sand that slid under my feet or even the clothes wrapped around my legs, promising to help me when I stepped over the shelf ahead, where the land surrendered to the sea and fell away.

I ran unfeeling fingers through the water, wanting to touch each drop that contained Matteo. When I gave myself up to it, I would be in each drop too.

I walked the last of the land, too afraid to go under but knowing all I had to do was take one step, then one more, in a final ritual. There would be no choice when I fell into darkness.

Confession

A hand grabbed my shoulder as I took my final walk through the waves, but I refused to turn. I knew it was Agatha, but the time to be sisters had gone. I was a danger to her, to them all. Before I had been only an embarrassment, a burden.

'Stop walking,' she said, her voice so ragged I knew she'd been calling it forever. 'Please,' she said, and it was the plea, not the order that stopped me. My big sister instructed, not begged.

'You can't do this.'

'I can,' I said. 'Finally, I can.'

'Then don't.'

'You want me in pain?' I asked.

'We're all in pain.' As she spoke a swell unbalanced us, and I took the arm grabbing me.

'I know it hurts,' she said. 'But you can't give up. Rosa, can you hear me?'

I had been staring at the water. 'It's all right.'

'How can this be all right?' Agatha said. 'It's nothing like all right.'

'This isn't giving up.' I slipped free, then out of reach, toward the ledge where I would drop away beyond rescue.

'Rosa, stop. Please,' she sobbed, but I had stopped once for begging. To do it again would give cruel hope.

'Ceecee is Matteo's daughter,' she said.

The string holding a kite snapped and cut me loose.

'My daughter is his daughter. Your niece is his child.'

As the wind twisted me, released, I saw Agatha's rigid face, as if the freed words had bitten her.

My stare asked questions. My voice clung to denial. 'No,' I said, breaking into a breath that curled away from me. 'Why would you say that? Did you think that would stop me?'

Agatha dared take a step closer, but I held up a hand. I didn't need to walk. I could fall into the sea right here if I let go. So I did, surrendering to the tug of the waves. There was no need to carry this, to live with it, to live at all. The water understood, pouring into my nose and mouth as I drifted to the seafloor. No more fighting. Just let go.

Agatha grabbed me. I lashed back. Couldn't she leave me be? I was so tired. Then I realised she was holding me while we both lay on the seabed. As children that's how we slept, drifting in a tangle of her and me with no line between.

Her eyes glittered in flashes of light from the surface, and I saw it exhausted her as much as me. We craved the silence of no more, and we could have it here, but I couldn't bring her with me.

I twisted and stood, clumsy and burdened, my breath a whimper as I broke the surface, and a cry when my sister took the hand I offered.

Truth in the Lie

My sister and I shivered in the listless sea, having failed to drown ourselves or each other.

'I cry every day,' she said. 'I look at my daughter.' Her voice faded. 'I love her. I do. But I cry.'

Even before she told me, I knew what my husband did those nights I watched him across the bay, when he waved as he left his boat, not saying he was going for a drink, letting me tell myself that. He was a liar who said less, planted seeds for me to nourish.

I knew not because I smelled perfume or strangers soap when he came home, but because I smelled no beer or rum. I kept that information from myself. It seems I saw the ghost of Matteo long before he died.

'That's why you never kept her from me?' I said, glancing at Ceecee on the shore. How else had a guileless child come to me under the eye of a watchful mother? Agatha didn't speak or look at me, and yet she had let her daughter visit.

She trembled a nod.

'How long?' I asked. The questions we ask that we don't want but need answered.

'Not long.'

'More than once?'

In the time she took to not answer, exhausted from the storm, the sea calmed around us.

'Why?' I said.

'I wanted to be you,' she said, sure of this. 'To dream, for just a moment. To act as if there were more out there, and no consequences here. I destroyed everything.'

'You left me alone.'

'I couldn't talk to you,' she said, 'You would have known.'

'I was alone.'

'I couldn't help you without hurting you more.'

'You couldn't hurt me more,' I said, and in that moment, that was true. I felt no pain, felt nothing.

I looked at the pearl in my hand. The first thing Matteo gave me. He lied before he spoke.

'You told me a pearl is a secret,' I said to the sea. 'But a pearl is a lie. A piece of dirt covered a thousand times until it looks beautiful, something people want to love. But it's still a piece of dirt, still a lie.' I dropped it, and it made no ripple.

'I put Ceecee in danger,' I said to my sister.

'You thought she was safe.'

'Because I had a straw man. Another worthless thing I wanted to believe.' I barked a laugh. 'The straw man drew the lightning. No one's safe in a storm.'

We looked to the shore, the broken house and people.

'I'm alive. You are and Ceecee is. Jacobo is. One of those boys is alive, and another isn't. Matteo is dead.' I said it out loud and to myself. 'The living must continue. That's all there is.'

'Must Jacobo know?' Agatha asked.

'Never. Nor Ceecee.' We agreed on that, each for our own reasons, as we waded back to the shore.

Ceecee ran from the hobbling man who'd raised her and threw her arms around us both. She might be the pearl that grew from the lie, but to have her hold me was proof we can grow beyond what made us.

Another Word for Love

The tide washed us with dirty white foam as we sat on the ruined beach, the corpse between us, before dawn but after night, too early for healing, too late for hope. We survived a storm and a fire but lost everything. I was a widow for a decade, while Sol's friend lay unburied, but grief is ever new.

I watched the sun's rays on waves that gave no hint of the ferocity stored in them. The furious colours of the storm turned gold then blue. Dead fish scattered amongst the logs and the debris of smashed boats. A net twisted on the line of a weary sea not strong enough to take it, too greedy to let go.

'Do they come back?' Sol asked me. He thought a widow would know.

'They don't come back,' I said, staring at the net. 'But we don't let them leave.'

'I didn't want this,' he said to Illy, then to me.

I twisted at a thin cry. A bird circling what had been my house. No more smoke rose from the broken walls, but the stench reached out.

'You had plans,' he said. 'Things you wanted to do?'

'We had plans,' I said. 'My man would bring me the world. Now I must go get it myself. He was a lie, so he made me a lie. You should tell your friend the truth while you can still remember it.'

'He can't hear me.'

'Whisper it in his ear.'

'He's not there.'

'But you are,' I said.

Sol leaned close to Illy, whispering through the filthy sheet, but I heard him. 'I let you go,' he said. 'When we were in the sea. I thought I'd save us both. Now we're both lost.'

Sol sat up, and we stared at the sea, clean now, after the destruction before.

'I don't want to whisper anymore,' Sol said.

'Then shout,' I said, remembering screams into thunder.

Sol laughed, surprising us both. 'He allowed me to shout. To roar, to run, to shout and jump. And now he's gone.'

'And you can't do those things anymore?'

'No.'

'Even though those were the things he wanted?' I asked.

'He's gone.'

'How can you not do the things he loved you to do?' I said, but he didn't answer, and I spotted the hollow in him. I'd not seen it in someone else before, but I knew it well. The step through a thin door to somewhere else. The escape into secret pathways between you and them, the missed and missing. I grabbed Sol's hand, digging my nails into him, forcing him back to this world, this beach, this dead man rotting between us.

'Let me tell you the one thing I know,' I said. My chest hurt as if I'd been sobbing. 'They are the bastards,' I said. 'They leave us all the pain. They can't do any more wrong. We stumble further and further away, making them perfect. But they weren't.'

'He was my friend.'

'Now he's at peace, and you're in agony,' I said, tearing the back of his hand as he pulled it from mine and took Illy's cold hand instead and squeezed it to his tears.

'Bastard,' he said, so his friend knew his love.

Sons

Sol watched Jacobo limp toward them across the wrecked beach. Over the years the older fisherman had become a leader, without ever seeming to try. He led the villagers at a solemn pace, not just because of his obvious discomfort but respectful of death and battered by the storm that brought it. Little Ceecee, not even ten years old, watched him unsteady on his cane, glancing back at her mother when he staggered.

Sol stood to face them. In the smiling way of the village, Jacobo was his enemy. One of those who drove his father from his home, with false friendship and sideways comments when he refused to fish after a tragedy at sea. That had been a vague phrase for Sol, more a story around him than something he lived through. Until now, when he stood by the drowned body of his best friend, Illy.

'I'm sorry,' Jacobo said when he reached him. 'We all are.' Sol saw him struggle for more words, knowing there were none, and he had none in return.

'We want him to come home,' Jacobo said at last. Behind him two fishermen carried a narrow canoe. 'We have a place ready. But if you prefer the sea to have him, we understand. You're the closest he had to family. But he was also a son of the village.'

Sol was used to Jacobo's eyes on him, watching for him and Illy to slip up, but now they searched him in a way he didn't recognise.

He looked down at Illy. Son of the village? The words sounded unreal in the new silence of the storm's wake. And yet he could see his friend, the peacemaker, with all of these people, nodding his easy-going smile.

He looked to the widow Rosa, but she couldn't help him. None of them could. These were the people he'd taken Illy from, to protect him from their hypocrisy. But what would he have wanted?

Sol stood aside, and the village understood. Each in their way, did their best to ease the burden. Women arranged the body in the canoe, covering the ragged, bloody shroud with a purifying white sheet. The men lifted it so they were pallbearers, with a space for Sol, which he stepped into.

When they reached the village in the bright, hard light, he saw how the storm had torn the tree from the earth, but also how it refused to fall, accepting support from the ropes the villagers pegged around it. The huge tree had protected them and their predecessors, now they would help it if they could. When Sol saw a grave dug under the exposed roots, he found he was holding the canoe for support, not carrying it.

Beside the grave a man stood with a soft cap in his hands. It took Sol several weak steps to recognise his father. The last time he'd seen him, Sol had been in the highest branches of that tree, refusing to leave the village.

'I asked him to come,' Jacobo said. 'When he left, he told me to keep an eye on you boys.' Jacobo's voice cracked when he said, 'I wish I'd done a better job.'

Everything tilted for Sol. He'd understood so little.

His father stepped in beside him, his arm over his shoulder. Together they lay Illy, the orphan who became their son, their brother, into the open space under the roots.

Sol's memories of that day never resolved. There were fractured conversations, silences that were more eloquent, and loss in abundance.

Ceecee came to the father and son, asking if they would help to haul the tree upright. That was how Jacobo had hurt his back, she explained, trying to hold the tree up on his own while the others got more rope. Her mother shushed her chatter, told her to go stand with her friend, Juan, but as she did it she kissed the little mop of curls on the girl's head with slow tenderness.

They added their hands to those on the ropes, guiding the tree as upright as it would go, packing the roots with new soil, sealing Illy underneath, so he could help it recover, become part of the village story.

Sol saw his father off again that night but from the ground, not the highest branch. They parted with a handshake and a promise to bring Sol's mother next time, to visit both her boys.

The Tree

That day, I watched the funeral procession walk back to the village behind Sol who shared the weight of his friend with others.

I stood to one side. The widow, the witch, the willing outcast from the village and my family. Neither the burnt remains of my house nor the sea called me.

My sister waited on the beach where I met my husband, where I came to find him when I lost him, the beach he walked across to be with her.

I took one step toward her, toward the village, and then another.

Today I sit, waiting under the crooked giant, which is what they call the tree now. The big storm was ten years ago. There have been others since, but we are better prepared. We rebuilt the pier. Put up proper defences. The sale of a piece of blue amber rescued from my house helped a little.

Music seems to drift in from the sea, but it's Sol, playing a battered guitar. It belonged to Illy, and he says it soothes him. He plays well.

Hearing the music, Ceecee leans on Jacobo's arm, and takes a step from her house. I see her adjust to the light through her white veil.

Ceecee and Jacobo walk toward us. They believe they are father and daughter, so they are.

The mother of the bride, my sister, grips my hand, so proud, though both she and I have cried more than once today.

The groom, Juan, looks handsome and uncomfortable in his suit. As Ceecee takes those slow and deliberate steps, I think of my Matteo, who waited for me one day, and left me another, who I walked after into the sea, but didn't drown for.

'I know that you're dead,' I say to him, and I know that it's true. I wish him well.

ACKNOWLEDGEMENTS

I'd like to thank the editors and readers at the flash journals who gave homes to my stories for all their work and encouragement. It's a great community and I'm delighted to be part of it.

Special thanks to the Bath Novella-in-Flash Award organisers, and *Ellipsis Zine*, particularly Stephanie Carty, for seeing the potential in *Straw Gods,* but most of all to David Borrowdale and Reflex Press for all the hard work bringing this book to print.

*

The author and publisher would like to think the editor of the *Bangor Literary Review* for first publishing 'Click, Click, Click' in October 2019.

OTHER TITLES FROM REFLEX PRESS

Some Days Are Better Than Ours
Barbara Byar

Some Days Are Better Than Ours is a startling collection that explores human life in all its forms. These stories will make you draw breath as you race through compelling accounts of the dark places people escape to and from.

Through her masterful use of language, Barbara Byar skilfully invites the reader into imagined futures and regretful pasts – from war to childhood to road trips to relationships. Her pieces are visceral, sometimes brutal but sliced through with hope. These stories, and the characters in them, strike straight at the realist heart of the human experience and will linger long after reading.

'These are searingly truthful fictions. Pitched at the border of poetry and prose, they catalogue lives lived at the edge, survivors facing the beauty and cruelty of the world. These fictions will take your breath away.'
—William Wall, *Suzy Suzy* and *Grace's Day*

'Barbara Byar writes flash like no one else; in each of these lucid and furious twenty-nine stories – some no longer than a single page – are wholly unforgettable glimpses into the lives of her individual characters.'
—Peter Jordan, *Calls to Distant Places*

Families and Other Natural Disasters
Anita Goveas

Families and Other Natural Disasters is a collection of flash fiction about families, born into, created or found, how they support us or repress us, and the ways they can change us and shape us.

These stories are set in the UK and India, in aquariums, ballrooms and outer space. They follow women into volcanoes and out to sea. The characters search for lost brothers and lost selves and find prairie dogs and sea serpents.

In a debut collection rich in cultural detail, Anita Goveas beautifully explores the theme of family as one of the essential elements that hold the universe together.

'Narratives that intersect continents, myths and folklore – a magical exploration of love, belief and the complications in relationships, with others and with oneself. Left me breathless and craving for more.'
—Susmita Bhattacharya,
The Normal State of Mind and *Table Manners*

'This gorgeous collection brims with energy and sensuality. Richly observed stories to catch the heart and quicken the pulse.'
—Sharon Telfer,
two-time winner of the Bath Flash Fiction Award

REFLEX PRESS

Reflex Press is an independent publisher based in Abingdon, Oxfordshire, committed to publishing bold and innovative books by emerging authors from across the UK and beyond.

Since our inception in 2018, we have published award-winning short-story collections, flash fiction anthologies, and novella-length fiction.

www.reflex.press
@reflexfiction